Kopecks for Blintzes

This **PJ BOOK** belongs to

_____

_____

PJ Library®

JEWISH BEDTIME STORIES and SONGS

To my dad, Berthold Goldman, who was so very proud of his people. — J.G.

KAR-BEN PUBLISHING
A division of Lerner Publishing Group, Inc.
241 First Avenue North
Minneapolis, MN 55401 USA
1-800-4-KARBEN

Website address: www.karben.com

Main body text set in Klepto ITC Std 15/20.
Typeface provided by International Typeface Corp.

Library of Congress Cataloging-in-Publication Data

Goldman, Judy, 1955- author.
    Kopecks for blintzes / by Judy Goldman ; illustrated by Susan Batori.
        pages cm
    Summary: "Yankl and Gitele live with their large family in Chelm, Poland. As Shavuot approaches, they decide to save coins in a giant wheeled trunk so they can make blintzes. But when both of them don't add their coins to the savings, a crazy chain of events leads the Rabbi to make three commandments just for Chelm"— Provided by publisher.
        ISBN 978-1-4677-7985-2 (lb : alk. paper)
        ISBN 978-1-4677-7987-6 (pb : alk. paper)
        ISBN 978-1-4677-9609-5 (eb pdf)
    I. Batori, Susan, illustrator. II. Title.
    PZ7.G5682Kop 2016
    [E]—dc23   2015016339

Manufactured in Hong Kong
1 - PN - 1/1/16

051621.9K1/B0820/A6

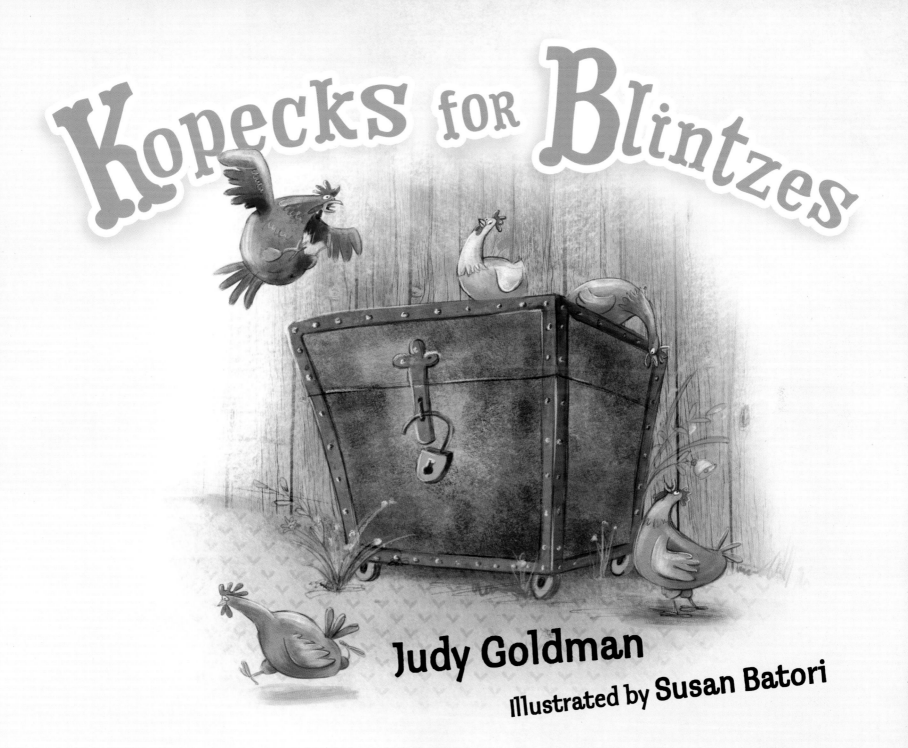

Kopecks for Blintzes

Judy Goldman

Illustrated by Susan Batori

KAR-BEN
PUBLISHING

Chelm was a small town like many in Poland, except for two very important differences.

The first was that the townspeople there were so foolish that they all believed they were the wisest people on the earth.

The second was that they had Thirteen Commandments instead of the usual Ten.

This is the tale of how they received three extra Commandments.

One evening Yankl and his wife Gitele were sitting in their tiny, slanted house at the top of the steepest hill in Chelm. All was quiet. Their many sons and daughters were asleep.

Yankl sighed deeply.

Gitele asked, "What's wrong?"

Yankl said, "In a couple of weeks it will be Shavuot. Everyone will celebrate Moses receiving the Ten Commandments. Just this morning, the rabbi reminded us that, because the Torah and the Commandments are sweet on the tongue, on Shavuot we should eat food prepared with milk and honey. That means blintzes! But we cannot afford ingredients for blintzes."

This was true. Yankl earned very little as a *melamed,* a teacher, and with so many children to clothe and feed, he and Gitele had little to spare.

Gitele sighed too. "If only we had a few coins. Then I would make the best blintzes!"

They sat lost in thought, imagining blintzes stuffed with cheese, smothered in sour cream, and dripping with honey or strawberry preserves.

Suddenly, Yankl jumped up. "I know what we can do!" he cried. "Remember that old trunk that my great-aunt Fruma gave us as a wedding gift?"

Gitele wrinkled her nose. "Who could forget it? It's so big and awful that it's been in the backyard since she gave it to us."

"That old trunk is going to solve our problem," said Yankl.

They ran to the backyard. Yankl examined the ugly, dirty trunk from all angles. Then he told Gitele his idea. "I'll make a small hole in the top of the trunk. Every day we'll each drop in a kopeck. In a couple of weeks, we'll open the trunk and use the coins to buy ingredients for blintzes!"

Gitele clapped her hands. "What an excellent plan! Yankl, you are one of the wisest men in this town."

Gitele and Yankl washed and cleaned the trunk and even greased the very squeaky wheels. When they finished, Yankl cut a hole in the top and dropped in a kopeck. Gitele dropped in a coin too. "We'll be eating blintzes in no time!" said Yankl.

The next afternoon, Gitele fished a kopeck out of her apron pocket and went to the trunk, ready to drop it in. But suddenly she thought, *Why should I put in a coin when Yankl brings home money from his teaching every day? Let him do it!*

So she put the coin back into her pocket.

That night, when Yankl came home, he searched in his vest pocket for a kopeck. He was about to drop it into the trunk when he thought, *Why should I put in a coin if Gitele will add one every day? She must have plenty of money left over after taking care of household expenses. With what she puts in, surely there will be enough for the blintzes.*

So he put the coin back into his pocket.

And this went on for several days.

On the morning before Shavuot, Gitele, Yankl, and their children gathered in front of the trunk. Yankl lifted the lid, and everyone peered in.

"We've been robbed!" gasped Yankl.

"*Gevalt!*" Gitele wailed. "Those thieves left us only two coins!"

But then, out of the corner of her eye, she looked at Yankl. "Tell me the truth, Yankl. Did you drop in your coins?"

"Well, no. I knew yours would be enough." Yankl's eyes widened. "You mean you didn't drop in your coins either?"

"Well, if you had put in *your* coins we would have had enough!" snapped Gitele.

Yankl groaned. "Now we won't eat blintzes, and it's all your fault!"

"If you weren't so stingy, this never would have happened!" Gitele yelled. She jabbed Yankl in the chest with her finger. He stepped back, tripped, and lost his footing.

"Help!" he cried, grabbing Gitele by her apron as he tipped over into the trunk.

Gitele fell into the trunk on top of him! The lid slammed shut, and slowly the trunk rolled out of the yard and down the hill.

As the trunk rolled onto the crowded street, it gathered speed.

"Oy, oy!" Yankl yelled.

"Gevalt! Gevalt!" Gitele shouted.

People scrambled to get out of the trunk's way. It narrowly missed an old woman, who made a sign to ward off the evil eye. "A *dybuk!*" she cried. "There's a demon in the trunk! I heard it yelling! The forces of evil have come to Chelm!"

A crowd of scared—but very curious—people ran after the trunk. At last it reached the bottom of the hill and rolled to a stop in front of the synagogue.

The rabbi, who had been decorating the synagogue with Shavuot greens, looked up in surprise. He approached the trunk and heard muffled sounds coming from inside. As he reached out to lift the latch, a man yelled, "Don't touch it, Rabbi! There are dybuks inside."

A woman added, "If they're let loose, we'll be lost!"

The rabbi's gentle face paled. He reached for his prayer book and turned page after page, looking for a prayer to banish the dybuks from Chelm. When he finally found it, he closed his eyes, swayed back and forth, and mumbled the words.

The townspeople stepped back—just in case the prayer hadn't done its job. Ever so slowly, the rabbi opened the trunk.

And out popped Gitele and Yankl!

Everyone stared. "How did you come to be in this trunk?" asked the rabbi.

When he had heard the story, the rabbi sighed. "Go home, everyone. This has been a terrible experience for all of us, so I must think of a way to prevent it from happening again."

The rabbi went to his study and consulted his books. All night he searched for an answer.

After a sleepless night he came to a decision.

The following morning, during Shavuot services, right after the Ten Commandments were read, the rabbi announced three new Commandments.

They were written in big black letters on a board and placed at the entrance to the synagogue.

And they are there still, reminding everyone that Chelm is home to the world's wisest fools.

AUTHOR'S NOTE

According to Jewish folklore, the people of the fictional town of Chelm (there is also a real town with the same name) were so clever that they never let sound judgment get in the way of a foolish idea. It is said that one day a long, long time ago, God chose two angels and gave one angel a sack of wise souls and the other a sack of foolish ones. God asked the angels to spread them out evenly all over the world, but the angel carrying the sack of foolish souls tripped over a mountain and—oy!—dropped them all into a town called Chelm. There the souls settled and, since then, every man, woman, and child that lives there is sure that they are the wisest creatures of the world, and can solve any problem with their sharp wits.

Judy Goldman was born in Mexico City, where she was brought up speaking Spanish and English and lived in a house filled with books. She has published over 40 books in Mexico, the United States, Colombia, Brazil, and Germany. She and her husband share their home—an apartment at the top of a mountain—with Sabrina, a Welsh Corgi. Judy loves animals, plants, writing, reading, and always carries a book with her wherever she goes.

Susan Batori is a Hungarian illustrator, graphic designer, and loves character design and creating new digital textures. She studied graphic design at the Hungarian Academy of Fine Arts, Budapest, Hungary. Susan is enthusiastic about macaroons, the color turquoise, and nature. She works in her small studio in Budapest focusing on children's book illustration.